P9-DOH-188

All Through My Town

Jean Reidy   illustrated by Leo Timmers

SCHOLASTIC INC.

No part of this publication may be reproduced, stored in a retrieval system, or
transmitted in any form or by any means, electronic, mechanical, photocopying,
recording, or otherwise, without written permission of the publisher.
For information regarding permission, write to Bloomsbury Children's Books,
1385 Broadway, New York, New York 10018.

ISBN 978-0-545-67558-1

Text copyright © 2013 by Jean Reidy. Illustrations copyright © 2013 by Leo Timmers.
All rights reserved. Published by Scholastic Inc., 557 Broadway, New York, NY 10012,
by arrangement with Bloomsbury USA Children's Books. SCHOLASTIC and associated logos
are trademarks and/or registered trademarks of Scholastic Inc.

12 11 10 9 8 7 6 5 4 3 2 1   14 15 16 17 18 19/0

Printed in the U.S.A.   08

This edition first printing, January 2014

Art created with acrylics
Typeset in Billy
Book design by Donna Mark

To Mike, my wingman on all my adventures,
whether they be halfway around the world
or just around the town —J. R.

For Gina, without whom I would be lost —L. T.

Rising, waking.
Bread is baking.
School bus honks its horn.

Seeding, sowing.
Rooster crowing.

Counting ears of corn.

Pancakes flipping.
Cutting, clipping.

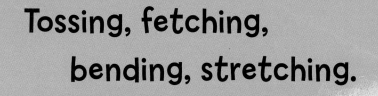

Tossing, fetching,
bending, stretching.

Brushing, shaving.
Good-bye waving—

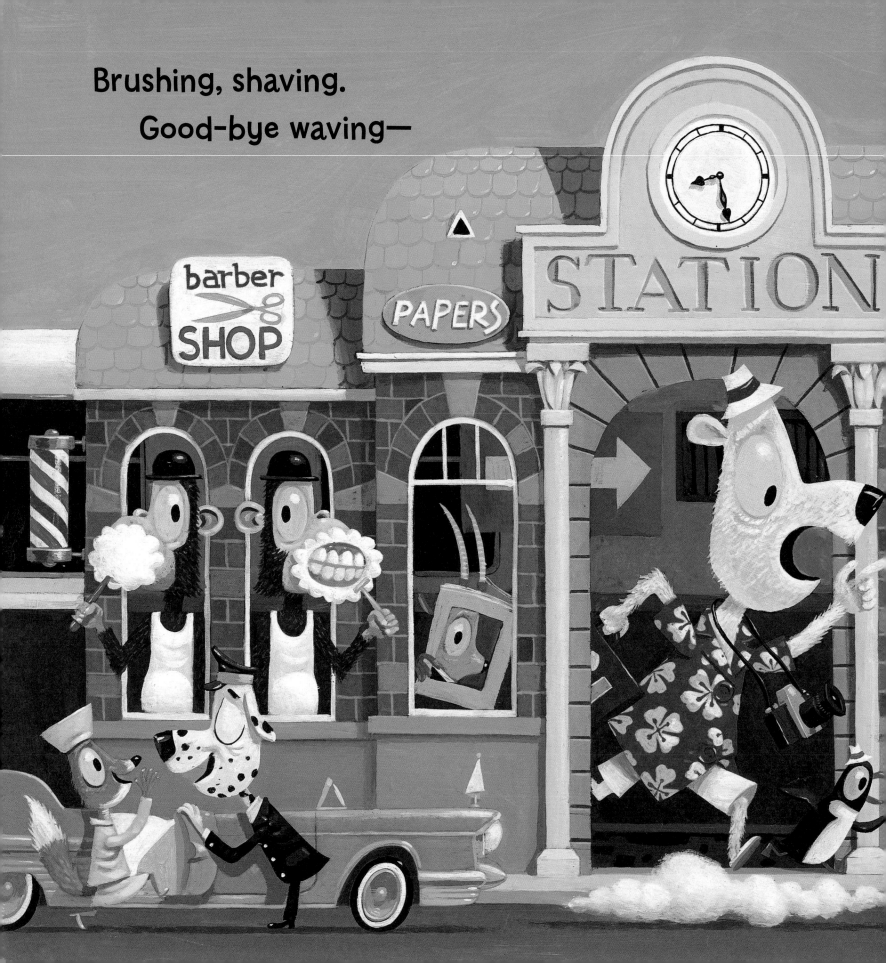

my town in the morn.

Shopping, sacking,
sorting, stacking—

rows so nice and neat.

School bells ringing.
Reading, singing,

friends to meet
and greet.

Spraying, sweeping,
backing, beeping.

Starting, stopping,
trolley hopping.

Blazing, dashing.
Red lights flashing!
My town's busy street.

Stamping,
mailing,
painting,
nailing,

ladder up and down.

Whistling, wheeling,
helping, healing.
Laugh away a frown.

Shelving, shushing.
Fountain gushing.

Swinging, lunching.
Cookie munching.

Peeking, peeping—
someone's sleeping . . .

All through my town.